INNOCENCE

INNOCENCE

The Life and Death of
Michelangelo Merisi,
Caravaggio

FRANK McGUINNESS

faber and faber
LONDON · BOSTON

First published in 1987 by
Faber and Faber Limited
3 Queen Square London WC1N 3AU

Photoset by Wilmaset Birkenhead Wirral
Printed in Great Britain by
Redwood Burn Ltd Trowbridge Wiltshire
All rights reserved

British Library Cataloguing in Publication Data

McGuinness, Frank
Innocence.
I. Title
822'.914   PR6063.A234/
ISBN 0-571-14917-0

for Philip Tilling and Patrick Mason

The life and death of Michelangelo Merisi, Caravaggio

CHARACTERS

CARAVAGGIO – Michelangelo Merisi, painter
LENA – friend to CARAVAGGIO
WHORE – friend to LENA
ANTONIO – rough trade
LUCIO – rough trade
CARDINAL – patron to CARAVAGGIO
SERVANT – to CARDINAL
BROTHER – Giovanni Battisti, to CARAVAGGIO
SISTER – Caterina, to CARAVAGGIO

Innocence was first performed at the Gate Theatre, Dublin, on 7 October 1986. The cast was as follows:

CARAVAGGIO	Garrett Keogh
LENA	Kate Flynn
WHORE	Pat Levy
ANTONIO	Peter Holmes
LUCIO	Joe Savino
CARDINAL	Aiden Grennel
SERVANT	Michael Ford
BROTHER	Jonathan Ryan
SISTER	Olwyn Fuore
Directed by	Patrick Mason
Designed by	Joe Vanck
Lighting by	Mick Hughes

LIFE

Music, Vespers, Monteverdi.
A circle of characters.
Detached from them, CARAVAGGIO *observes, fingering a skull.*
LENA *caresses a red cloak, like a child.* ANTONIO *and* LUCIO
caress each other. WHORE *rocks herself to and fro, weeping.*
CARDINAL *recites the Offertory from the Tridentine Mass, holding a*
host. SERVANT *kneels at* CARDINAL's *feet, with* BROTHER.
SISTER *moves through the circle, repeating her prayer.*

SISTER: Thine, O Lord, wilt ope my lips and my tongue shall
announce thy praise. Incline unto my aid, O Lord. O Lord,
make haste to help me.

(*Wrapping the red cloak about herself,* LENA *moves to comfort*
WHORE. ANTONIO *and* LUCIO *kiss.* CARDINAL *raises the*
host in elevation. SERVANT *and* BROTHER *fall prostrate before*
it. CARAVAGGIO *raises the skull.* LENA *tears the red cloak from*
herself. Sounds resembling the Latin from the Mass start to pass
among the characters. The cloak starts to stretch about them.
The noises increase, breaking into animal sounds, eventually
becoming a horse going mad, as the cloak now moves wildly
through the characters. CARAVAGGIO *approaches the*
cloak-horse, holding the skull before the wild shape.
CARAVAGGIO *touches the shape with the skull. The shape*
screams. It wraps itself violently around CARAVAGGIO. *Hands*
start to beat him. CARAVAGGIO *falls, roaring. Darkness.*

Light. A hovel. LENA *examines a red cloak.* CARAVAGGIO
sleeps, a bandage around his eyes. A skull lies on the floor
beside him. CARAVAGGIO *wakes up with a start.*)

CARAVAGGIO: Where am I?
LENA: So you're back among the living?
CARAVAGGIO: What have you put on my eyes, woman?
LENA: What'll cure you. Why?
CARAVAGGIO: Nothing.
LENA: Had my little goat a bad dream?
(CARAVAGGIO *spits.*)
LENA: Touchy, touchy.

I

(CARAVAGGIO *searches for a goblet on the floor.* LENA *throws the cloak aside.*)
That's perfect now. We should invest in a new cloak. I can't keep up repairing this. It's as old as I am. I'm sick seeing the same old ball-covering every time you take a fancy for a fucking John the Baptist. You should learn to sew, you know that? (CARAVAGGIO *finds the goblet.*) Might keep the cup out of your hand.
(*She reaches for a mirror.*)

CARAVAGGIO: Fill this, will you?
(*Silence.*)
Lena?
(*Silence.*)
Lena, where are you?
(*Silence.*)

LENA: Jesus, I'm getting old.

CARAVAGGIO: Old?

LENA: Old. Wrinkled. Past it. (*She wails.*)

CARAVAGGIO: Yea.

LENA: I'm not that past it.

CARAVAGGIO: Yea, give us some wine.
(*Silence.*)
Look, I pay for my fair whack of the booze in this kip, so where is it?

LENA: I hid it.

CARAVAGGIO: Did you? Fetch it.

LENA: You can wait. You're not getting a drop until you compliment me. Compliment me.

CARAVAGGIO: You look grand.

LENA: No. I don't. I look old. I am old.

CARAVAGGIO: Jesus, preserve me.

LENA: It's terrible to grow old.

CARAVAGGIO: Jesus, protect me.

LENA: You don't notice it happening and it happens.

CARAVAGGIO: Right. Two can play at this game, baby.

LENA: No, shut it, Lello. Listen to me.
(*She sits by* CARAVAGGIO.)

CARAVAGGIO: OK, we're off.

LENA: I was in Navona today and I saw a midget.

CARAVAGGIO: My name is Michelangelo Merisi.

LENA: She had a hump, the midget.

CARAVAGGIO: Michelangelo Merisi da Caravaggio.
(*He strokes* LENA's *back.*)

LENA: I swear to Christ I looked at her and she was happier than me – hump and all.

CARAVAGGIO: Michelangelo for the angel and not for that chiselling cocksucker.

LENA: No worries, not a line on her face. Do you know why? What did a man ever matter to a woman like that?

CARAVAGGIO: (*Stroking* LENA's *face*) Merisi for my family and Caravaggio for the birthplace of my father.

LENA: I don't blame men. I lead the life I want to lead but that midget, she'd have been as content in a convent as me – me content? Where would I be content, Lello?

CARAVAGGIO: (*Continuing to stroke* LENA's *face*) I paint with my hands as God intended the eyes to see and to see is to be God, for it is to see God.

LENA: I should have entered a convent.
(CARAVAGGIO *embraces* LENA.)

CARAVAGGIO: In all Rome I stand supremely alone as painter, seer and visionary, great interpreter of man.

LENA: I'd have been happier in a convent.
(*She pushes him away.* CARAVAGGIO *raises his hands.*)

CARAVAGGIO: I take ordinary flesh and blood and bone and with my two hands transform it into eternal light, eternal dark.

LENA: Better than this dump.

CARAVAGGIO: For my art balances the beautiful and the ugly, the saved and the sinning.

LENA: I wonder do convents take midgets.
(*She lays her head on* CARAVAGGIO's *lap.*)

CARAVAGGIO: I am the great Caravaggio and I am keeping up this shit for as long as I need to until I am poured a bloody drink.
(*He kisses* LENA.)

LENA: I mean I'm no midget but I feel at times as if I've a

3

hump. Maybe it's not too late to become a nun. I was mad
about Our Lady when I was a girl. Christ, would you
believe that? I used to imagine I was her daughter and Jesus
was a right pup who tormented me. The innocence of it.

CARAVAGGIO: (*Running his hands along* LENA's *body*)
I paint as I see in light and as I imagine in darkness, for in
the light I see the flesh and blood and bone but in the dark
I imagine the soul of man for the soul and the soul alone is
the sighting of God in man and it is I who reveal God and it
is God who reveals my painting to the world.

LENA: (*Sitting up*) What in under Jesus are you rabbiting on
about, Lello?

CARAVAGGIO: I am Michelangelo Merisi da Caravaggio, called
Lello by cretins, who do not know that he with whom they
dare to be familiar works with his hands, paints with his
hands, and his hands are the hands of God alone.

LENA: Lello, should I enter a convent?

CARAVAGGIO: You have the hump for it. (*He laughs.* LENA
walks towards him.)
What are you doing?
(LENA *puts her hand down Caravaggio's trousers.*)
What are you doing?
(LENA *starts to masturbate* CARAVAGGIO.)
I hate women doing that to me.

LENA: I am Michelangelo Merisi da Caravaggio.

CARAVAGGIO: For Jesus' sake, Lena.

LENA: My genius is recognized all over Rome.

CARAVAGGIO: I'm a defenceless man.

LENA: I am Michelangelo Merisi and I am a wanker.

CARAVAGGIO: Lena.
(LENA *pulls* CARAVAGGIO's *cock roughly.* CARAVAGGIO
yelps.)

LENA: That was the hand of God.

CARAVAGGIO: You're a rough woman.

LENA: I've had to be. Fend for myself. That's what happens
when you've never had a husband.

CARAVAGGIO: A beautiful woman like you?

LENA: A beautiful woman like me.

4

CARAVAGGIO: No husband?

LENA: No.

CARAVAGGIO: Not married?

LENA: No. Never married.

CARAVAGGIO: Do you want to?

LENA: Get married?

CARAVAGGIO: Why not?

LENA: Don't know. (*She pours them some wine.*)

CARAVAGGIO: Bit dangerous always, this game.

LENA: I love this one. Keep going. Here's wine. Keep going.

CARAVAGGIO: You know where it might lead to.

LENA: Look, is this or is this not a proposal?

CARAVAGGIO: What do you think?

LENA: It's a bit sudden. I mean, I hardly know you. You better take me out walking first.

CARAVAGGIO: Where?

LENA: A girl can't be too safe. Tell me about yourself. Your people, who are they? Who's your father?

CARAVAGGIO: Dead. He's dead.

LENA: And your mother?

CARAVAGGIO: Dead.

LENA: Are you from Rome?

CARAVAGGIO: No. From Caravaggio. But I had to leave.

LENA: And do what?

CARAVAGGIO: See the world.

LENA: Why?

CARAVAGGIO: What?

LENA: See.

CARAVAGGIO: I like seeing.

LENA: I trust you, let's go somewhere.

CARAVAGGIO: Where?

LENA: Somewhere on our own. Somewhere secret. Somewhere beautiful.

CARAVAGGIO: There's a forest.

LENA: The forest, yes.

CARAVAGGIO: It's very dark. Will you be afraid?

LENA: Yes, but I like the dark.

CARAVAGGIO: Why?

5

LENA: Why do you like seeing?

CARAVAGGIO: I like the forest, even if it's dark, because you can still see in it always.

LENA: The animals.

CARAVAGGIO: The birds.

LENA: The trees.

CARAVAGGIO: The leaves.

LENA: Do you see them?

CARAVAGGIO: Yes.

LENA: Do you know their names?

CARAVAGGIO: Sometimes. Do you want children?

LENA: How many?

CARAVAGGIO: Ten?

LENA: Twenty.

CARAVAGGIO: A hundred?

LENA: Thousand.

CARAVAGGIO: Million.

LENA: One.
> (*Silence.*)
> Cut it.

CARAVAGGIO: What's his name?

LENA: Not tonight. Leave it.

CARAVAGGIO: All right.
> (*Silence.*)

LENA: You on the prowl tonight?

CARAVAGGIO: Yea, I better. His eminence has the hot horn again. I've been a bad boy.

LENA: How?

CARAVAGGIO: Been neglecting him.

LENA: What way?

CARAVAGGIO: Between one thing and another.

LENA: Watch yourself there. A nice line going. We need the financial blessing of father church.

CARAVAGGIO: We?

LENA: We, sweetheart. Go easy with the Cardinal, boy. Your bread has cheese on it there.

CARAVAGGIO: I'll do what I like where I like when I like.

LENA: It's like talking to a stone.

6

CARAVAGGIO: That's right.

(WHORE *enters, notices the silence. It persists.* CARAVAGGIO *fingers the skull.*)

WHORE: I love coming into this house. You're so pleasant always.

CARAVAGGIO: Remember, woman, thou art dust and unto dust thou shalt return.

WHORE: That bandage suits you. Why don't you get one for your mouth? Oh, is that wine?

CARAVAGGIO: Lady, I wouldn't give you my wine even if there was poison in it.

WHORE: And I wouldn't piss on you if you were on fire.

LENA: I hate to interrupt this sparkling repartee but why are you in here?

WHORE: Would you ever give us the lend . . .

LENA: No.

WHORE: You don't know what I was asking –

LENA: Money. You're not getting it.

WHORE: I'm not looking for money. I want a lend of your gold ribbon. The one he got you.

LENA: That's the best stitch I possess.

WHORE: Don't be so selfish. When you went on the streets first, I was like a mother to you.

LENA: You robbed me of every penny you could get your hands on.

WHORE: Exactly. Money ruins young ones. A mother knows that. Lend us the ribbon.

LENA: No.

WHORE: Give us a drink then.

CARAVAGGIO: No.

WHORE: I get the decided feeling I'm not wanted.

CARAVAGGIO: Remember, woman, thou art dust and unto dust thou shalt return.

WHORE: Will you stop saying that to me?

CARAVAGGIO: Remember, woman, thou art dust and unto dust thou shalt return.

WHORE: Fit you better if you said your prayers.

CARAVAGGIO: Thou art full of grace and the Lord is with thee. Blessed art thou among women.

7

WHORE: Blessed. I know, I know. Blessed.
(*Silence.*)
CARAVAGGIO: What's the difference between you and a barrel of shite?
WHORE: What?
CARAVAGGIO: The barrel.
WHORE: Mock on, mock on, God sees you. He hears you. I'm not getting the ribbon?
LENA: You're not.
WHORE: All right. Thank God I didn't ask to borrow a dress. You never know when he might want to wear it. Be good, Lena. You can't be much else with his kind, can you? I'll leave the holy family in peace.
CARAVAGGIO: May you die roaring.
WHORE: Ciao. (*She exits. Silence.*)
CARAVAGGIO: When can I take this fucking cloth off my eyes?
LENA: When I say so. I had to eat Rome to get the right herbs. The last time you hadn't the patience to lie still in the dark till they were half-way healed. I learned my lesson if you didn't. Coming crying to me. I'm going blind, Lena. I won't see. I won't paint. What's going to become of us?
CARAVAGGIO: Well I am a bloody painter and a great one.
LENA: You're a dirty shit and a long one.
(CARAVAGGIO *moves to tear the bandage from his eyes.*)
Don't dare put your paws near that bandage till I tell you, I'm warning you.
(CARAVAGGIO *pulls the bandage from his eyes. He roars with pain.*)
CARAVAGGIO: It stings.
LENA: Pity about you.
CARAVAGGIO: My eyes are burning out of me.
LENA: God love you.
CARAVAGGIO: For Christ's sake, Lena, do something.
LENA: Such as?
CARAVAGGIO: You're the healer, you know.
LENA: Sorry, can't help.
CARAVAGGIO: Have I done myself permanent damage?
LENA: Who knows? You're the big man. You know it all.

8

CARAVAGGIO: Tell me the truth, cow, the truth.

LENA: Moo, moo.

CARAVAGGIO: I'm not laughing, Lena.

LENA: Mooo.

CARAVAGGIO: Do something.

LENA: Mooo.

(CARAVAGGIO *draws his knife.* LENA *rises and hits him.*)

CARAVAGGIO: Jesus.

LENA: You snivelling pup.

CARAVAGGIO: I'm sorry.

LENA: Who the hell do you think you are? Who do you think you are dealing with? Some penny piece of pansy rough you scraped off the streets? By Jesus, boy, you should know better than to try that caper.

CARAVAGGIO: I'm sorry.

LENA: You should know a damn sight better.

CARAVAGGIO: I shouldn't have done it. I know. I'm sorry.

LENA: Such an action.

CARAVAGGIO: It was the first time.

LENA: And last time you'll try it with me, whoever else you might terrorize.

CARAVAGGIO: I'll make it up to you.

LENA: How much?

CARAVAGGIO: Not with money. I'll paint you.

LENA: You've painted me, goat.

CARAVAGGIO: Not for a long time. I haven't painted you as you are.

LENA: Yea, the whore.

CARAVAGGIO: No. Beautiful and angry. Lena. Look. Watch. Lena.

LENA: Yea, Lena the whore.

CARAVAGGIO: No, girlfriend.

LENA: Girlfriend, yea.

CARAVAGGIO: Girlfriend to the goat, to Caravaggio.

LENA: My dream goat.

CARAVAGGIO: Dream goat.

LENA: Unicorn.

CARAVAGGIO: Dream.

LENA: Unicorn.

(*Their foreheads touch.*)

CARAVAGGIO: Forest.

LENA: Forest.

(CARAVAGGIO's *fingers start to touch* LENA's *face.*)

CARAVAGGIO: A bird moves through the forest. A golden bird,
and the bird is golden because it carries the sun. The bird sees
the tree and it feeds the tree with sun. The tree feeds the leaf,
and the leaf loves the tree, and the tree cradles the bird and
Lena is the bird who is the sun and the tree and the leaf, for the
leaf is the fruit of the beautiful earth. I gather the earth's fruit
and the tree's leaf and I plant them in your face for your face is
a bowl full of life, full of Lena. Here, Lena, look, your face.

(CARAVAGGIO *holds out his hands to* LENA. *They caress her
face and hair, returning to her face. Then he holds out his hands
before his own face, admiring them.*)

Your face. Yes, Lena, your beautiful face. (*He blows his
nose into his hands.*)

LENA: Get out.

CARAVAGGIO: You fall for it every time, wagon.

LENA: Out.

CARAVAGGIO: I suppose a ride's out of the question?

LENA: You should be so lucky, queer.

(CARAVAGGIO *moves to exit, grabbing the cloak as he leaves,
while* LENA *hurls the skull after him. He catches it.*)

LENA: Don't bring that fucking skull into my house, it watches
me.

(CARAVAGGIO *exits,* LENA *shouting after him.*)

Jesus, am I glad I put pepper into that eye mixture.

CARAVAGGIO: (*Off*) Whore.

LENA: Goat.

(*Silence.* LENA *moves back to the hovel. She lifts up the
bandage, scowls, smiles. She throws aside the bandage, picks
up the mirror, looks into it, removes it from her sight.*)

I wonder where's the nearest convent.

(*Fade.*

The street. ANTONIO *and* LUCIO, *rough trade, wait.*

ANTONIO *bites his nails.*)

LUCIO: Stop biting your nails.

ANTONIO: I'm hungry.

LUCIO: It's a rotten habit and it's bad for you.

ANTONIO: So's whoring.

LUCIO: So?

ANTONIO: So I'm hungry. I bite my nails. Want a bite?

LUCIO: Fuck off.

(*Silence.*)

I have really long nails. Really nice. Well, so I've been told.

ANTONIO: Mine are disgusting. I think that's why I eat them. Get rid of them.

LUCIO: This ponce I picked up once, nice bastard, he said to me I had fingers that were carved. He said they had the flow of a musician's hands, they should have an instrument in them. I told him they often had. He didn't think it was funny. Queers have no sense of humour.

ANTONIO: I have.

LUCIO: You are not a queer. You might be a whore for the sake of your belly but you're no queer. I wouldn't hang about with you if there was anything wrong with you.

ANTONIO: I like men.

LUCIO: Don't be disgusting.

ANTONIO: I like their arses. I like biting them. That's what's really wrong with me. My mouth always has to be doing something. Maybe if I'd been born deformed, without a mouth or something, I'd be married. I do know I wouldn't always be hungry.

(*Silence.*)

I do think I've a sense of humour though.

LUCIO: Who said you hadn't?

ANTONIO: You did. You said queers –

LUCIO: You are not –

ANTONIO: I'm bent as a nail. So are you.

LUCIO: Well don't go saying it. Bad enough doing it.

ANTONIO: And we're not doing it.

LUCIO: Funny enough I noticed that.

(*Silence.*)

I hate being poor.

ANTONIO: I know. Hunger drives you mad. I saw a ghost last night.

LUCIO: I think I'll cut out this caper. It's no work for a man.

ANTONIO: It had no head on its shoulders and it knew my name.

LUCIO: Get a woman or something. This crack can't last for ever.

(*He starts to do press-ups.*)

ANTONIO: I wasn't dreaming either. It really had no head, this ghost. I let one roar out of me.

LUCIO: Women would be less fussy. I suppose there's more of them. There's more women than queers, aren't there?

ANTONIO: Do you know what really scared the life out of me? I thought this ghost must be my father or my mother.

LUCIO: Yea, I'm going off the game. I'm packing this in. I'm packing it in tonight.

(*He stops doing press-ups.*)

ANTONIO: So I bent down to pick it up, the head, and see exactly who it was and it bit me.

LUCIO: What bit you?

ANTONIO: The ghost bit me.

LUCIO: Ghost?

(*He kisses* ANTONIO.)

ANTONIO: It started to speak. It blamed me. It said I cut off its head.

LUCIO: Whose head?

ANTONIO: The ghost's, my father or mother.

LUCIO: How? They're dead.

(*He rubs* ANTONIO's *hair.*)

ANTONIO: That's why I thought they must be the ghost, stupid. I started to cry. It laughed. No head, and it was laughing. Have you ever heard anything that weird?

LUCIO: Are you in one of your visions?

ANTONIO: I couldn't believe the sound of it. A ghost laughing.

LUCIO: Who are you talking to?

ANTONIO: God.

LUCIO: Why?

ANTONIO: I'm lonely.

LUCIO: Talk to me then.

ANTONIO: Why should I?

LUCIO: Why shouldn't you?

(*Silence.*)

ANTONIO: Will we try the last resort?

LUCIO: We tried it last night. Don't want to overdo it.

ANTONIO: It didn't work last night.

LUCIO: He mustn't have heard us.

ANTONIO: So will we do it?

(*They kneel.*)

LUCIO: You pray.

ANTONIO: Hear us, Father in Heaven.

LUCIO: We're hungry.

ANTONIO: We could eat each other.

LUCIO: Not that. Say something religious.

ANTONIO: Such as?

LUCIO: This is my body.

ANTONIO: This is my blood.

LUCIO: Turn me into bread, God.

ANTONIO: Me into wine.

LUCIO: Give us a miracle.

ANTONIO: Give us a man.

LUCIO: Not even that. Work a reverse job. Flesh and blood into bread and wine.

ANTONIO: Give us a feed, Lord, if it's only ourselves.

LUCIO: Wait a minute, what if he hears us?

ANTONIO: He never hears us.

LUCIO: But if he does, we're fucked.

ANTONIO: That's the general idea.

LUCIO: Send us a man, God.

ANTONIO: Send us your son.

LUCIO: He was a god.

ANTONIO: Send us a god then, we're desperate.

LUCIO: Don't talk like that. It's a sin. It makes me nervous.

ANTONIO: So?

LUCIO: He'd strike us down dead if he hears us.

ANTONIO: He never hears us.

LUCIO: There is a first time for everything.

(*Silence.*)

13

ANTONIO: Do you remember the first time?

LUCIO: No.

ANTONIO: I do. What age was I? Thirteen or fourteen?

LUCIO: I remember. I called you my little brother. You were beautiful.

ANTONIO: Thank you.

LUCIO: Keep it down. See your man.

ANTONIO: Where?

LUCIO: Watching.

ANTONIO: No.

LUCIO: Standing in the dark. Can't make him out too clearly. Taking in everything though. Wait for the moon to catch him.

ANTONIO: We'll be here all night.

LUCIO: Think he has a beard. Can't see all his face, but a thick-looking customer. I see him. Give you a hiding as soon as look at you. Face like a horse's arse.

ANTONIO: Fuck it, he'll fancy me. Why me always with the dreamboats?

LUCIO: Oh Jesus, I think it's the pervert.

ANTONIO: What's wrong with that?

LUCIO: This boy is something special.

ANTONIO: Know him?

LUCIO: Had him.

ANTONIO: We're safe?

LUCIO: Strung to the moon.

ANTONIO: What did he do?

LUCIO: Never said a word the whole night. Let me rattle on and plied me with drink. Then the props appeared.

ANTONIO: Oh Jesus, for a beating?

LUCIO: No.

ANTONIO: Then what were the props?

LUCIO: Grapes.

ANTONIO: Grapes?

LUCIO: Barrels of them.

ANTONIO: Now that is different. Grapes.

LUCIO: He squeezed grapes all over me. There was even a bunch hanging from my balls. Then he ate them. I have a

14

good stomach but I swear I nearly took sick. He started to call me Bacchus.

ANTONIO: Who the hell's Bacchus?

LUCIO: How the Jesus do I know?

ANTONIO: Probably some boyfriend he had one time, foreign with that name. There's ones like that.

LUCIO: I haven't told you the best bit yet.

ANTONIO: What?

LUCIO: He had me dress up.

ANTONIO: As a woman?

LUCIO: As a fucking tree.

ANTONIO: How a tree?

LUCIO: Leaves all over my head, right? Rotten old fruit dripping all over me. He had fire burning all about me. My big red cheeks burning like two beetroot. Jesus, I felt a right prick.

ANTONIO: Were the grapes still around your balls?

LUCIO: No, I told you he ate the grapes.

ANTONIO: What was the fire for?

LUCIO: It was the dead of night and he wanted light to see me. The bastard's a painter. He was painting me.

ANTONIO: As a tree?

LUCIO: As Bacchus.

ANTONIO: Oh yes, Bacchus. Is he a lunatic?

LUCIO: He's a painter.

ANTONIO: Does he pay OK?

LUCIO: I can't remember.

ANTONIO: Oh come on.

LUCIO: I was pissed out of my head when he had me. My skull was flying.

ANTONIO: And you were that drunk you didn't remember if he paid?

LUCIO: I was younger then.

ANTONIO: Well, he's still watching.

LUCIO: He's all yours.

ANTONIO: Are you sure?

LUCIO: Positive. If he wanted the two of us, he'd have made a move before now. I'll shift. Keep me a bunch of grapes.

ANTONIO: Wait.

15

LUCIO: He's for you, Antonio.

ANTONIO: I don't like the cut of him, Lucio.

LUCIO: He pays well, Toni darling. We need the money.

ANTONIO: But you said you couldn't remember if he –

LUCIO: I remember he pays.

ANTONIO: Don't leave me yet, Lucio, please.

LUCIO: Pansy, fucking pansy. Why do I bother?

ANTONIO: Please, big brother.

(CARAVAGGIO *enters.*)

LUCIO: Fine night.

(*Silence.*)

The mate here was just remarking on the moon. A man should enjoy a moon like that. What do you think yourself?

(*Silence.*)

Are you taking a stroll like ourselves?

(*Silence.*)

I'm heading for my kip. This boy, you couldn't stop him wandering. He's making for a last trip to the river.

ANTONIO: Don't believe him. I'm not. I never hang around the river.

LUCIO: What are you saying?

ANTONIO: We're not bent. Don't beat us up.

LUCIO: He won't do that, will you?

ANTONIO: We better get home, Lucio.

CARAVAGGIO: You share a home?

ANTONIO: Yes. The wife will be waiting up for us.

CARAVAGGIO: You share a wife?

ANTONIO: Yes.

LUCIO: No. We live by ourselves. Do you feel like joining us?

CARAVAGGIO: Join me.

(CARAVAGGIO *puts a gold coin into his hand, holds it out towards* LUCIO, *who goes to snatch the coin.* CARAVAGGIO *grabs* LUCIO *by the hair.*)

Gold.

(CARAVAGGIO *throws more coins on to the ground and points at* ANTONIO.)

You as well. Come on.

(*He exits.* LUCIO *rapidly collects the coins.*)

LUCIO: Come on. Follow him.

ANTONIO: Go home with what we've got. Give him the slip, Lucio.

LUCIO: For Jesus' sake, there's more where that came from. Come on, Antonio. (*He exits.*)

ANTONIO: Lucio.

LUCIO: (*Off*) Come on.
(*Silence.*
ANTONIO *moves to exit, pauses.*)

ANTONIO: See you, God, you're a right bastard. Good luck. (*He exits.*
Fade.)

The palace of CARDINAL *Francesco del Monte. Tapestries and paintings. A bench. Cushions on the floor. Meat on a gold platter. A bowl of fruit.* CARAVAGGIO *carves meat with his knife, the red cloak beside him.* LUCIO *and* ANTONIO *watch* CARAVAGGIO *eat, as they drink wine.* ANTONIO *raises the bowl of fruit and approaches* CARAVAGGIO, *offering him the food.* CARAVAGGIO *grunts refusal.* ANTONIO *turns to go.* CARAVAGGIO *signals him to stay and watches him holding the bowl, rearranging his hand and pulling Antonio's shirt from his shoulder to expose the flesh.*
ANTONIO *waits patiently after* CARAVAGGIO's *attentions.*
CARAVAGGIO *grunts* ANTONIO's *dismissal.* ANTONIO *shrugs and approaches* LUCIO *with the bowl of fruit, lifting before* LUCIO's *face a bunch of grapes.*

ANTONIO: Memories.
(LUCIO *laughs.*)

CARAVAGGIO: What?

LUCIO: How quickly they forget.

ANTONIO: All the same, men. The whole lot of them. Only after one thing.

LUCIO: Animals.

ANTONIO and LUCIO: Thank Jesus.
(*They laugh, directing the joke at* CARAVAGGIO *who does not respond. Silence.*)

ANTONIO: What's your name anyway?
(*Silence.*)

17

He thinks he knows you.

(*Silence.*)

LUCIO: Can I have some food?

CARAVAGGIO: Why didn't you ask before? Are you shy or
something?

LUCIO: Why didn't you offer it?

CARAVAGGIO: Not mine to offer.

LUCIO: Whose is it then?

CARAVAGGIO: Your buyer.

LUCIO: You're not the buyer?

(*Silence.*)

You a pimp?

(CARAVAGGIO *throws wine into* LUCIO's *face.*)

CARAVAGGIO: Sorry. (*He refills his wine cup.*)

ANTONIO: You're a rough man, aren't you?

CARAVAGGIO: No. (*He offers* LUCIO *meat.*) You starving as well?

(ANTONIO *nods.*)

Eat. Share it.

(*They jump on the food.*)

Eat like Christians. Where's your manners in the priest's
house?

LUCIO: Christ, are you a priest?

CARAVAGGIO: No, I'm a saint. I know what Rome's like. Easy
to be waylaid by your like. I travel disguised.

LUCIO: As what?

CARAVAGGIO: Guess.

LUCIO: A woman?

(CARAVAGGIO *laughs.*)

A beard works wonders for a woman.

ANTONIO: Can women be saints?

LUCIO: Shut up, you stupid bastard.

ANTONIO: I only asked.

(*Silence.*)

CARAVAGGIO: What makes you think I'm a priest?

ANTONIO: You have loads of money.

LUCIO: The way you move your hands. And they're clean.

ANTONIO: Are they? I love clean hands. Give us a look. (*He
examines* CARAVAGGIO's *hands.*) They're really hard.

18

CARAVAGGIO: Soft. Not hard. Soft. (*He looks at* LUCIO.) Soft. Like your face used to be.

ANTONIO: No, they're not that clean, not scrubbed like.

LUCIO: So you remember?

ANTONIO: I mean, I've seen cleaner.

CARAVAGGIO: I never forget a face.

LUCIO: Even when you paint it?

ANTONIO: The hands are a dead giveaway for age.

CARAVAGGIO: Clever boy. Strange boy.

ANTONIO: Yea, dead giveaway.

CARAVAGGIO: Strange.

(*Silence.*)

ANTONIO: Nice place you have here, father.

CARAVAGGIO: I'm not your father. Don't call me that.

ANTONIO: You said it was a priest's —

CARAVAGGIO: I'm nobody's father.

(*Silence.*)

LUCIO: Who's the buyer?

CARAVAGGIO: A rich man.

ANTONIO: Is he nice?

CARAVAGGIO: He's rich. All rich men are nice. Right?

ANTONIO: Right. Great. He pays well?

CARAVAGGIO: Extremely well.

ANTONIO: Great.

LUCIO: How do you know him?

CARAVAGGIO: He's my buyer too.

LUCIO: What does he do?

CARAVAGGIO: To live?

LUCIO: Yea.

CARAVAGGIO: Prays for your soul before claiming your body.

LUCIO: Is he a young guy?

CARAVAGGIO: You like them young?

LUCIO: Do you not?

CARAVAGGIO: He's young at heart.

LUCIO: I hate old men. They smell like fish. They should be gutted and fed to each other.

ANTONIO: Pathetic old bastards.

LUCIO: Slice the wrinkled old shits to ribbons.

ANTONIO: Slowly.

CARAVAGGIO: With what? Slice them to ribbons with what?

LUCIO: My nails.

> (LUCIO *imitates an animal clawing.* ANTONIO *follows suit. They mock-fight about the room.* CARAVAGGIO *enters their game, encouraging them.*)

CARAVAGGIO: What are you?

> (LUCIO *roars.*)

Lion.

> (LUCIO *leaps on* CARAVAGGIO *who avoids him.* LUCIO *reaches for the tapestries and tears at them with his teeth.*)

Hound.

> (LUCIO *bays like a hound.*)

ANTONIO: Can I be something too?

CARAVAGGIO: Hare. Gentle hare.

ANTONIO: Just a hare?

> (CARAVAGGIO *pats* ANTONIO. LUCIO *turns into a wild horse, attacking* ANTONIO, *who squeals.* CARAVAGGIO *throws him off* ANTONIO, *and as* LUCIO *kicks out,* CARAVAGGIO *touches his face.*)

CARAVAGGIO: Steed, trusty steed.

> (LUCIO *rises again, breathing fiercely, following* ANTONIO.)

LUCIO: I'm no steed. I'm a dragon, and this is fire.

CARAVAGGIO: Fly, boy, fly. Turn into a bird, a fighting bird. An eagle.

> (ANTONIO *turns into an eagle, landing on* LUCIO's *face.* LUCIO *bellows like a bull.*)

Bull.

> (ANTONIO *and* LUCIO *turn into fighting bulls. As they fight,* ANTONIO *calls to* CARAVAGGIO.)

ANTONIO: What are you?

CARAVAGGIO: Lizard. Poisonous lizard. Creeping on you. Touching you. Kissing you. Poison. Touching. Kissing. Poison. Kissing. Kissing.

> (ANTONIO *and* LUCIO *fear the lizard.*)

Calm, calm, my animals. Come to me. Calm.

> (ANTONIO *and* LUCIO *come quietly towards him.*)

Unicorn, unicorns, calm. (CARAVAGGIO *captures* LUCIO *and*

ANTONIO *gently. He holds them both.* ANTONIO *breaks away first for more wine. He brings* CARAVAGGIO *the bowl of fruit.*)

ANTONIO: That was great.

(CARAVAGGIO *looks at* LUCIO's *hand. He examines* LUCIO's *fingernails.*)

LUCIO: Taste.

(CARAVAGGIO *puts* LUCIO's *finger into his mouth and chews it gently.* LUCIO *removes the finger and* CARAVAGGIO *kisses it.* LUCIO *touches* CARAVAGGIO's *face. He starts to trace the outline of* CARAVAGGIO's *scar.*)

What's the mark on your face?

(*Silence.*)

Is that why you have the big beard? To cover the mark? Where did you get the mark?

CARAVAGGIO: It was worse once than it is now.

LUCIO: Near your eyes. Were you almost blinded?

CARAVAGGIO: I couldn't see much after it, but what I saw, I saw clearly.

LUCIO: You were kicked in the face.

CARAVAGGIO: How do you know?

LUCIO: It wasn't from a human.

CARAVAGGIO: What from then?

LUCIO: An animal. So was I. Years ago.

(LUCIO *bares his thigh to show a wound.* CARAVAGGIO *touches it.*)

CARAVAGGIO: Horse.

LUCIO: Horse. I fell. I scared it. It kicked out. It got me.

ANTONIO: I was bitten by a rat once.

LUCIO: Were you riding the horse?

ANTONIO: Bit on the ear. I couldn't hear for a month in it.

CARAVAGGIO: It was wild.

ANTONIO: Nobody listens to me.

(ANTONIO *lies at* CARAVAGGIO's *feet, playing with fruit in the bowl.*)

CARAVAGGIO: I tried to save it.

LUCIO: What from?

CARAVAGGIO: Itself. I have a way with animals. Innocent at heart. Even the wildest.

21

ANTONIO: A black rat it was too. It was in my bed. I felt a lump by my leg. I thought I was asleep. But I felt it move. Crawling beside me. Black.

CARAVAGGIO: I thought I was blinded.

ANTONIO: I shot roaring out of bed. I hoped it was a lizard. But it was a rat. It ran like mad.

(*He curls himself up, closer to* CARAVAGGIO.)

CARAVAGGIO: I thought this will be the last thing I see. A horse.

ANTONIO: The rat was probably more scared than I was, but that's no consolation.

LUCIO: But it wasn't.

(CARAVAGGIO *strokes* LUCIO *and* ANTONIO.)

ANTONIO: My father heard me crying. He lifted me up. Right into his arms. I could never remember him touching me before. I felt all his strength. I loved that.

(*He kisses* CARAVAGGIO's *hand*.)

CARAVAGGIO: For the first time I saw.

ANTONIO: Then he dropped me when he found out why I was crying. He shouted about plague. He threw me into a barrel of rain. It was cold.

(*He releases* CARAVAGGIO's *hand*.)

CARAVAGGIO: It touched me, the horse. It saw me. And I could see its touch.

LUCIO: What about touching people?

ANTONIO: I thought I was going to drown. My father wouldn't save me. He didn't want me. He never had.

CARAVAGGIO: Seeing. Touching.

(*His eyes closed,* CARAVAGGIO *tries to touch* ANTONIO.)

ANTONIO: I couldn't hear myself crying but my face was wet. I thought I was deaf. Maybe he was deaf too, my father. Maybe he couldn't hear me crying either.

LUCIO: Are you afraid of touching?

(*Silence.* ANTONIO *starts to beat the ground with the gold platter, scattering meat.*)

ANTONIO: I'm going to get married. Married to a woman, a woman would hear you. Men only hear what they want to hear. Like my father. I hate them. I was bitten by a rat. My father held me. I went nearly deaf. I'm all right now. I can hear. Listen to me.

LUCIO: You prepare yourself for the buyer.

ANTONIO: He's the buyer, you stupid bastard. He'll do the paying. And he wants you. It's always you. And you said he was mine. But you sit there fucking him with your eyes and hands and ears and every part of you but what counts and you know why you can't do that? Because the horse kicked the life out of them. Your balls are as much good to a man as a cunt.

LUCIO: What are you calling me?

ANTONIO: I'm sorry, Lucio.

LUCIO: If you want him, take him.

ANTONIO: Do you want me?
(*Silence.*)
Do you not want me?
(*Silence.*)
Who are you?
(*The tapestries open.* CARDINAL *appears, attended by a servant.*)

CARDINAL: Caravaggio. His name, my son, is Caravaggio.
(ANTONIO *and* LUCIO *kneel in the presence of the* CARDINAL.)

CARAVAGGIO: Michelangelo Merisi da Caravaggio, your eminence. And I bring these poor boys to your exalted presence. Feel them. Rough and ready, but to your taste. Bit of sweaty salt to savour the flesh. I know what you want, master. I give your eminence service as painter and as pimp and his eminence knows me as a good servant.

CARDINAL: You are more than usually distressed, Caravaggio. I hope I have not interrupted your little intrigue too early, my friend.

CARAVAGGIO: Do not honour me as friend, eminence. I am your humble servant. (CARAVAGGIO *lifts both boys.*) Receive my gift, cardinal. Caravaggio presents his offerings before his master, most high prince of the church.
(CARAVAGGIO *throws* ANTONIO *and* LUCIO *at* CARDINAL's *feet.*)

23

Rough, eh? Like me, no? Take us as you fancy. But I warn you your eyes are bigger than your belly. Your eyes want the lump of tough meat, but your belly needs refinement.

CARDINAL: I wish you would occasionally defy your reputation.

CARAVAGGIO: Eat and be merry, prince, tomorrow we die. Tonight, we die. All life is death, all light is darkness, and from the darkness your boys have crawled to bring you the light of love.

CARDINAL: You never cease to surprise.

(CARAVAGGIO *bows*.)

CARAVAGGIO: My only desire is to please his eminence.

CARDINAL: Poor eminence to have such a disruptive servant. I forgive you. Your behaviour distorts you. I'm afraid you lack – what is it they say? Charmingly vigorous, painfully natural, but lacking perspective? Perhaps not. No, you lack the perfect sense of detail that distinguishes the exceptional from the good. I believe they call what you lack discretion. You mouth shoots too much poison, Caravaggio. Take care it's not spat back.

(*Silence*.)

Sit down.

CARAVAGGIO: No peasant would sit in the company –

CARDINAL: You bore me, Caravaggio. Give me wine.

CARAVAGGIO: You heard his eminence. Respect the church. Respect old age. Give the prince his due. Give the old man your wine. (*He grabs Antonio's wine cup*.) Give his dry mouth your cock.

ANTONIO: Father – , eminence – , we –

CARAVAGGIO: Don't be ashamed. That's what he'll come round to asking you for. A little more time. A little more discretion. A little more work on it. Then it will be perfectly all right. I know what he wants. How could I not? I serviced him myself when nothing younger was about. I've given him my best. He knows it. He thanks me. He feeds me. He clothes me. And underneath it all I'm a good boy. I know the value of his money. I do as I am told. Painter and pimp. Painter to Cardinal del Monte, pimp to the Papal Curia, whore to the Catholic church. And they

24

need me. For I'm a very special whore. The cardinal is envied for his whore's expertise. Jesus, what I get up to with these hands has to be seen to be believed.

CARDINAL: If my memory serves me, I asked some time ago for something to drink.

(*On all fours* CARAVAGGIO *crawls to a wine cup and carries it back in his mouth to* CARDINAL. CARDINAL *laughs, takes the cup, gives* CARAVAGGIO *his ring to kiss.* CARAVAGGIO *kisses, then pours* CARDINAL *wine. He sits at* CARDINAL's *feet.*)

Excuse my fool's manners. He has not welcomed you as friends. Have you visited with him here before?

CARAVAGGIO: No.

CARDINAL: Where did he find you?

CARAVAGGIO: In church.

CARDINAL: At prayer?

CARAVAGGIO: Deeply.

CARDINAL: Good. Your spiritual grace matches your physical beauty. Come here. Sit by me.

(*Silence.*)

Come on.

(*Silence.*)

What are you afraid of? Of Caravaggio? Has he attacked you already?

ANTONIO: Yes, father.

CARDINAL: Lucky boy, eh, Caravaggio?

(CARAVAGGIO *bays like a dog.*)

He's on the leash here. He can only bark. No need to fear him. He has no power in my house. I am a man of God. My house is the house of God. You have no more need to fear me than you should fear God. Would God despise you for your poverty and your profession? No. Do I despise you? No. Come here. Sit. Both of you, sit. You, bring the bowl of fruit.

(ANTONIO *goes to* CARDINAL *with fruit bowl.* CARDINAL *selects fruit and eats. Softly*) Good boy. Sit down. Are you afraid of me as well?

ANTONIO: No, father.

(CARDINAL's *arm enfolds* ANTONIO. ANTONIO *cuddles towards him.*)

25

CARDINAL: Don't fear my animal either. An interesting animal. He likes to be punished. When he remembers his station, he's the best creature on God's earth. Aren't you, Caravaggio? Stroke him, don't be afraid.

(ANTONIO *strokes* CARAVAGGIO's *hair.*

Silence.)

Give me your knife, Caravaggio.

(CARAVAGGIO *gives his knife to* CARDINAL, *who holds it before* CARAVAGGIO's *face.*)

Look at him. Hear his breathing. Don't be afraid. Look. He carries this weapon but when he makes it my weapon, it could remove his sight for ever. Cut the eye from its socket. Slice the old bastard into ribbons. We know what excites you, Caravaggio? Blood. Can we see blood? If this knife moves into your eyes, what will you be? Where will you be, Caravaggio?

(CARAVAGGIO *squeals.*)

Is he so afraid? Is it so easy to terrify the wild Caravaggio? Yes, he has his peasant's fear of the dark. It's full of ghosts. Were you boys afraid of the dark when you were children? So was Caravaggio. He's still afraid and not just of the dark and its ghosts. Fear, Caravaggio. Poor Caravaggio. Cry with fear. Cry for me. Cry. (CARDINAL *slaps* CARAVAGGIO's *face.*)

LUCIO: Leave him.

CARDINAL: Take back your knife. No fun tonight. These boys, why have you chosen them? Was it for their dirt? Shave him clean. Wash him with your blade.

(CARDINAL *hurls* ANTONIO *from him.* CARAVAGGIO *leaps on* ANTONIO. ANTONIO *screams. To silence the scream* CARAVAGGIO *grips* ANTONIO's *throat.* CARAVAGGIO *raises the knife.* LUCIO *stays* CARAVAGGIO's *hand.*)

LUCIO: No.

(CARAVAGGIO *laughs.*)

CARAVAGGIO: Poor lambs. Has the big, bad wolf put the fear of God into your innocent souls?

LUCIO: Let us go home.

ANTONIO: Please, father. We have the money he gave us. We'll give it to you for masses or something.

26

LUCIO: We need that money.

CARAVAGGIO: Well said. Oh for Christ's sake, you've been in worse places.

LUCIO: You've recovered your senses, have you?

CARAVAGGIO: A miracle. Thank God for it. Go and offer thanks for saving your lives. This palace is full of chapels. Say your prayers in one before the entertainment starts.

CARDINAL: Remove them.

(*The* SERVANT *moves towards* ANTONIO *and* LUCIO.)

CARAVAGGIO: (*Sotto*) Don't forget to say your prayers.

CARDINAL: Bathe them.

ANTONIO: Let us go home, father.

CARDINAL: Clean them.

CARAVAGGIO: God will provide easy pickings.

ANTONIO: Let us go home.

(SERVANT *leads* ANTONIO *and* LUCIO *out*.)

CARDINAL: You'll be the death of me, Caravaggio.

CARAVAGGIO: I hope not, Cardinal.

CARDINAL: Why do you keep coming back here? Have you started to enjoy playing my fool?

CARAVAGGIO: I'm not a fool.

CARDINAL: Then you still must fear me. Why?

CARAVAGGIO: Yours is the hand that feeds.

CARDINAL: You would have bitten it off long ago if that's all it does. Why do you fear my hand? Why, Caravaggio?

CARAVAGGIO: Blesses. Yours is the hand that blesses. I fear that blessing and I need it. For I have sinned. And I sin. And I will sin. Forgive me.

CARDINAL: A dangerous man, aren't you, Caravaggio? You believe with a depth that is frightening. And with a vision that is divine. Don't think I am ignorant of your vocation. You believe, and since you believe you are chosen, not commissioned. I know you. I know you, Caravaggio. That's why you fear me. The painter of the poor. Dirty feet, rags, patches, kneeling in homage to their Virgin Mary, another pauper, mother of their God. And they know it and you know it. Who is this God? Why is it them he has chosen? The beloved poor who will always be with us, just as their

27

God will be with them, not with us. You remind us of unpleasant truths, Caravaggio. For that you may be hated. Your sins may be condemned. But you will be forgiven, for you are needed. Forgiven everything eventually. Dangerous words. A dangerous man. Saving himself by the power of his seeing. And by his need to tell what he sees. Tell me your sins. Confess, Caravaggio.

CARAVAGGIO: I saw two boys.

CARDINAL: And you led them astray from God's word.

CARAVAGGIO: One looked out at me, listening, and I watched him looking. Their shirts were white. The body underneath was brown. I could hear the white of their shirts touch their flesh. I knew they could see me listening in the dark.

CARDINAL: Did they speak?

CARAVAGGIO: I heard them whispering and laughing. I watched them touch each other. Still young, still desired, and I was angry. I was jealous. They were as near to me as you are, but in their youth and desire they were as far away as the stars in the sky. I wanted to raise my fist and grab them from the sky and throw them into the gutter where I found them. I wanted to dirty their white shirts with blood. I wanted to smash their laughing skulls together for eternity. I wanted the crack of their killing to be music in my ears. I wanted them dead. I wanted red blood from their brown flesh to stain their white shirts and shout out this is painting, this is colour, these are beautiful and they are dead. They are not there. The sin, not there. My sin, not there. Just my painting, not my sin. I didn't touch them. I did not kill them. I desired them. Oh my God, I am sorry for having offended Thee for Thou art the chief good and worthy of all love.

(*Silence.*)

CARDINAL: What am I to do with you, Caravaggio?

CARAVAGGIO: Do you not accept my sorrow?

CARDINAL: I always believed you were alone in this life.

CARAVAGGIO: I am.

CARDINAL: You told me in another confession you were an only child and your parents died many years ago.

CARAVAGGIO: Yes, I told you.

CARDINAL: You had a visitor today.

CARAVAGGIO: Who?

CARDINAL: You've asked for forgiveness. Sometimes to forgive is to punish. I think on this occasion God would declare that your punishment is to meet your visitor.

CARAVAGGIO: Who?

CARDINAL: A fellow priest. I let him wait for you. He claims to be your brother.

CARAVAGGIO: I told you I have no living family.

CARDINAL: Why have you lied?

CARAVAGGIO: He's the liar. I have no brother.

CARDINAL: He claims otherwise. Extraordinary, isn't it? Most interesting. I've given you the courtesy of asking him to wait until you were fully informed of his arrival. I shall be your servant, Caravaggio. I'll bring your brother to you. (*He exits.*)

CARAVAGGIO: No. No brother. No father. No mother. Dead. I have no brother. I do not lie. I tell the truth. I paint the truth.
(BROTHER, *Giovanni Battisti Merisi, enters with* CARDINAL.)

BROTHER: Why have you kept me waiting so long, Michelangelo?
(CARAVAGGIO *turns his back.*)
Don't turn your back on me.
(*Silence.*)
I've come here to see you.

CARAVAGGIO: You've seen. Leave.

BROTHER: Our sister, Caterina —

CARAVAGGIO: I have no sister. No brother. No father. No mother. Nobody belonging to me lives. I had a brother. He died and was buried.

BROTHER: Will you leave us together, your eminence?

CARAVAGGIO: I won't be left alone with this liar.

CARDINAL: He says he is your brother. I believe him. He is a priest.

CARAVAGGIO: He's a thief. Tell it by looking at him. A man like that is out for what he can get. Believe me, I have no brother. I do not lie.

(BROTHER *shows* CARAVAGGIO *his right hand. Around it are strung the beads of a black rosary.* BROTHER *unwinds the beads and holds them before* CARAVAGGIO.)

BROTHER: Our sister wanted you to have these.

(*Silence.*)

Our sister, Caterina.

CARAVAGGIO: No.

BROTHER: You know whose they are.

(*Silence.*)

Michelangelo.

CARAVAGGIO: No brother. No mother. I have no – I have no – Brother I have none. Leave.

(CARDINAL *reaches to look at the beads.* CARAVAGGIO *grabs them from* BROTHER's *hands. He buries his face in them.* CARDINAL *bows to them both and exits.*)

What do you want here?

BROTHER: You.

CARAVAGGIO: For Jesus' sake.

BROTHER: We didn't know if you were living or dead.

CARAVAGGIO: I'm living.

BROTHER: I see.

CARAVAGGIO: How did you track me here?

BROTHER: I heard you'd found a good patron.

CARAVAGGIO: Oh Christ, so that's it. Well at least you're to the point. My Giovanni, you never stop, do you? Never miss a trick.

BROTHER: That is despicable.

CARAVAGGIO: You crawled on your slimy stomach to worm your way into this palace. The brother's a painter, great favourite of his eminence, let me kiss the ring and put a good word in for me where it counts because that's a contact worth developing there, boy, am I right? Fuck off. You're neither needed nor welcome. Find another back to scratch.

BROTHER: Stop denying me like this. Why are you doing it?

CARAVAGGIO: Because dear brother, you are a lying, thieving bastard.

BROTHER: Remember my calling. I would remind you the priesthood –

30

CARAVAGGIO: And I would remind you I have been up the arses of more priests . . .

BROTHER: Shut your filthy mouth.

CARAVAGGIO: Don't come crying to me with your holy face, bastard.

BROTHER: Do not call me bastard. Bastard is one word you won't spit at me. You must think little of your own if that's what you have to throw at them.

(*Silence.*)

CARAVAGGIO: Brother.

(*Silence.*)

How is Caterina?

(*Silence.*)

I'm asking about our sister.

BROTHER: Caterina prayed long and sore for you.

CARAVAGGIO: She might save me yet. She misses me?

BROTHER: She forgave you.

CARAVAGGIO: Always. Did she marry?

BROTHER: She married.

CARAVAGGIO: Children?

BROTHER: Yes.

CARAVAGGIO: Beautiful, like her?

BROTHER: Yes.

CARAVAGGIO: Healthy, strong, like the Merisi breed?

BROTHER: Like the Merisi.

CARAVAGGIO: Good, good, Caterina. Are they boys, beautiful boys?

BROTHER: Has it sunk to this?

CARAVAGGIO: What?

(*Silence.*)

Jesus, do you think that?

(*Silence.*)

Do you really think that?

(*Silence.*)

You must really hate me. All my life I thought it was me who could hate. But it's you. You think that's why I ask after my sister's children?

BROTHER: I'm sorry.

31

CARAVAGGIO: You should be.

(*Silence.*)

No. Spare your sorrow, keep it for our nephews. They'll need it. I hope their father is a good man. Jesus they have a right pair of uncles, kid. You a eunuch, and me a cocksucker. (CARAVAGGIO *laughs.*)

BROTHER: Don't call yourself that.

CARAVAGGIO: It's true, isn't it?

(*Silence.*)

Christ, I believe you're going to start crying for me.

BROTHER: No, I'm not.

CARAVAGGIO: You did before.

BROTHER: I was too young when you told me about yourself. I didn't know enough. And you cried as well.

CARAVAGGIO: I've stopped.

BROTHER: So have I.

(*Silence.*)

CARAVAGGIO: Seen any of my work?

BROTHER: The paintings? Yes.

CARAVAGGIO: Good?

(*Silence.*)

BROTHER: The Cardinal is proud of them.

CARAVAGGIO: Why shouldn't he be? Do they not appeal to you?

BROTHER: They would appeal more to the initiated.

CARAVAGGIO: The Cardinal is certainly that.

BROTHER: Are you ashamed of them?

(*Silence.*)

Are you ashamed of them as well?

CARAVAGGIO: As well?

BROTHER: As you are ashamed of yourself. You always have been. I only cried, Lello, because you cried.

CARAVAGGIO: Thank you.

BROTHER: And you want me to be ashamed as well. That would give you a perfect reason to live as you live. Hard man. Dirty mouth. Filthy morals. It won't work with me. I won't give you the satisfaction of shocking me. I never will. I know my brother. That's why I've come to see you. I want a straight answer to what I have to ask you.

32

CARAVAGGIO: Risk it.

BROTHER: Come home with me. To our home. To our father's house.

CARAVAGGIO: It's yours. Keep it.

BROTHER: Get out of Rome. You'll die here. Look at you. An old man already. Why? No, I don't want to know why, but I do know you must leave this palace behind. Disease and dirt, that is what's here for you. Come home. Live clean. I want you.

CARAVAGGIO: Do you ever think beyond the edge of that hole you call home? Do you think it has any hold on me now?

BROTHER: Then why take your name from our village, Caravaggio?

CARAVAGGIO: Because I carry too much of it with me. I carry enough of it to know why I hate you.

BROTHER: Lello.

CARAVAGGIO: Jesus, man, what did you do to me years ago? You swindled me out of what little was left to me after Mama died.

BROTHER: No.

CARAVAGGIO: Don't deny that. I let you do it. Why the fuck do you think I let you grab what was mine for half-nothing? Do you think I would have given up without a fight if I wanted any place in the pit called home? You got it all, to do as you saw fit. It's all yours, father Giovanni, and you're welcome to it. Come home, me? Tell me where I'll find it first. I don't know. But I do know it's not where I was born.

(*Silence.*)

BROTHER: Come with me.

CARAVAGGIO: No.

BROTHER: Caravaggio.

CARAVAGGIO: No.

BROTHER: Home, Michelangelo.

CARAVAGGIO: No.

BROTHER: Merisi. (BROTHER *grabs* CARAVAGGIO's *hands*.)

CARAVAGGIO: I will not live on your land.

BROTHER: Take it. It's yours. Come home.

CARAVAGGIO: Go. Go.

BROTHER: Lello.

CARAVAGGIO: Go.

BROTHER: Mama.

(CARAVAGGIO *weeps*.)

CARAVAGGIO: I'm dirty. Very dirty.

BROTHER: Be clean. Come home.

CARAVAGGIO: Mama.

BROTHER: Home.

CARAVAGGIO: Mama dead. Clay, her feet in the clay. Dirty, in the grave. Dead. Wanted to die. Lonely. Mama.

(BROTHER *embraces* CARAVAGGIO.)

BROTHER: Lello, don't let us die with you, brother. Merisi, as you love our name, love me, protect me always. Protect our family. I had to take your inheritance for I knew you would sell it to the first bidder for a pittance. You sold it to me, to me, not a stranger. I've kept it for you until you were ready to come home.

CARAVAGGIO: Leave the priesthood. Father a child. A son. Healthy sons, plenty of healthy sons. Save our father's name.

BROTHER: There's still the lump of the peasant in you.

CARAVAGGIO: We have land. Who will it pass to but another man's sons if you don't breed?

BROTHER: I'm forbidden.

CARAVAGGIO: So am I. (CARAVAGGIO *disengages himself from* BROTHER'*s embrace*.)

BROTHER: Our father's land.

CARAVAGGIO: No, priest.

BROTHER: Breed.

CARAVAGGIO: I won't.

BROTHER: Can't?

CARAVAGGIO: Can't.

BROTHER: So you are what you say you are?

CARAVAGGIO: Yes, no, yes, no, yes, yes.

BROTHER: Stay where you belong, stay in the pit of sinners. You paint like a drunkard sees. Badly. It's as if you're asleep. All in the dark. A drunk man imagining in his

34

dreams. Who listens to a drunk roaring? Who looks at him? Noise. You're full of noise. Nothing but noise. You'll leave nothing behind.

CARAVAGGIO: My sister has sons. Caterina's sons.

BROTHER: Caterina is dead. The second son killed her at birth.
(CARAVAGGIO *stuffs his hands into his mouth*.)
She called for you with her dying breath. To remember her. That's why I searched for you. I hoped God had heard her. I thank God she didn't live to see what she had prayed for. Don't come near her sons.
(CARAVAGGIO *chokes on his fingers*.)
Don't come home. Your father died. Caterina died. Your mother is buried. Your brother dies before your eyes. It's as you wished. Your family is dead. You are no one.

CARAVAGGIO: I am Michelangelo Merisi da Caravaggio. I am Caravaggio. I am Michelangelo Merisi. I am my brother. I am my sister. My sister –
(*Silence*.)
My dead sister.
(*Silence*.)
Caterina, I'm afraid of death.
(BROTHER *exits*.)
Giovanni, my brother, don't leave me in the dark. I'm afraid of the night. Mama, don't haunt me. I'll say my prayers. I'll pray for you, sister. Come back to me alive. Come out from the shadows. Take me back. Let me see.
(*He finds a jug of wine and pours it into himself. He tears tapestries and paintings from the wall, ransacking the room.* LUCIO *and* ANTONIO *enter, dragging a bag of booty.* LUCIO *surveys the room*.)

LUCIO: Jesus, man, you should not drink on your own. His eminence will have a fucking fit.

CARAVAGGIO: Let him have his fit.

LUCIO: The haul in here is something else, boy. Wait till you see what we landed.

ANTONIO: Come on to hell, get out quick.

LUCIO: Wait a minute. You know the best place to get rid of good stuff at a fair price?

35

CARAVAGGIO: Yes.

LUCIO: Would you look after us?

CARAVAGGIO: I've the knife.

LUCIO: And you'd use it?

(CARAVAGGIO *slashes something*.)

That's what I love about you. You're so demonstrative.

ANTONIO: Lucio, could I have a word with you?

LUCIO: No.

ANTONIO: Your man's mad.

CARAVAGGIO: Trust me.

LUCIO: We trust you.

ANTONIO: Did you not see?

LUCIO: I see.

(ANTONIO *has noticed the red cloak. He stuffs it into the bag*.)

CARAVAGGIO: So do I. I see clearly. I see this knife. I see the hand that carries it. I curse my hand. I curse my life. I damn my soul. Trust me. (*He exits. Fade*.)

DEATH

Lena's hovel.
The WHORE *slumps across a table.*
LENA *dries her hair. A pitcher of perfume stands on the ground near her.* LENA *goes and shakes the* WHORE *awake.*

LENA: Come on, Anna. Rise and shine.

WHORE: No. Too tired. Sleep.

LENA: Sleep it off somewhere else. You've had a fair snooze here. Shift yourself. I'm not your nursemaid.

WHORE: No, Lena, it's warm here. Let me be.

LENA: I'm not running a lodging-house. You staggered in here, now stagger out.

WHORE: I'm tired, no.

LENA: Oh Christ, I give up. I'm too exhausted to argue. Perch there for the night. Don't try to stretch your way into my kip though, do you hear? Sleep where you are.

WHORE: No, you have me wakened now. I won't sleep.

LENA: Then I will, goodnight.

WHORE: Don't leave me.

LENA: Are you afraid of your own company?
(*Silence.*)

WHORE: Did I tell you who I saw this evening?

LENA: You were too drunk to stand, let alone talk.

WHORE: I was not drunk. I was transfixed. I saw a vision. I saw Our Lord. Our Saviour Jesus Christ. He appeared to me.

LENA: That's the second time this month. He's getting to be a regular.

WHORE: Don't be disrespectful. I met him after hearing mass. Suddenly he was standing before me. Suffused with a golden light. God love him, he showed me the big wounds in his side and his stomach. He let me put my fist into them. They were as big as your boot. I don't know how he survived the beating they gave him.

LENA: He didn't.

WHORE: No, I suppose he didn't. He gave me a message. A secret message.

LENA: What?

39

WHORE: I can't tell you. It has to be revealed only to the Pope and he has to tell it to the world. So I can't tell you. Only the Heavenly Father can do that. Anyway it doesn't exactly affect you, or me for that matter.

LENA: Then why tell you?

WHORE: He must have taken a liking to me. Nice-looking man. Very tall. Strong fella. Black hair, very thick, but a bit long. Lovely spoken. Do you want to know what the secret message is?

LENA: I don't want to spoil things between you and the Pope.

WHORE: I can tell you, Lena, for you know when to keep your mouth shut. He said to me, and this is strictly between ourselves, that whenever a Pope dies, he goes straight to Heaven. No fear of purgatory nor Hell for them. We always have a living saint on the throne of Peter. Isn't that great news for them? Jesus is delighted with their great work and he's chosen me to pass on the information.

LENA: I'm going to my bed.

WHORE: Stay up and keep me company.

LENA: Get to your own kip.

WHORE: What house or home have I? Nobody wants me. Not even you.

LENA: Not at this hour of the night.

WHORE: I taught you everything when you first started on the game. I looked after you. Now I'm only a burden.

LENA: I know.

WHORE: I'll die and nobody will miss me. No one will notice me gone. They won't even bury me.

LENA: Maybe you'll rise again on the third day.

WHORE: I'll be fed to the dogs.

LENA: They'll die of alcoholic poisoning.

WHORE: Laugh away. Some day you'll be my age –

LENA: And I'll die of alcoholic poisoning.

WHORE: Have you anything in the house?

LENA: Why do I open my big mouth?

WHORE: Maybe a night-cap would help us sleep.

LENA: I don't need help to sleep.

WHORE: Nonsense, I insist. Where is it?

40

LENA: No, you've had enough.

WHORE: The day I've had enough, they'll be fishing me out of the river after drinking it dry. Where is it?

CARAVAGGIO: (*Off*) Lena.

WHORE: Who the hell is that?

LENA: Clear out of here, woman.

CARAVAGGIO: Lena.

WHORE: If it's a client, he might go for the older type.

LENA: Just leave.

WHORE: Fuck off, Lena. I deserve my chance. You have the pick and choice.

CARAVAGGIO: Jesus, let me in.

LENA: Leave.

WHORE: No.

LENA: Then sit there and say nothing.

CARAVAGGIO: Lena.

(LENA *exits*.)

WHORE: I wonder where she hides the drink?

LENA: (*Off*) Where are you? I can't see you in the dark. Oh Christ. Lello. Get water. Do you hear me, Anna?

WHORE: What?

LENA: Water. Bring him in. (LENA *enters*.) Bowl and water. Quick. Cloth as well.

WHORE: All right. What for?

LENA: Bring it.

(CARAVAGGIO *enters, supported by* LUCIO. *He is wounded in the back of the head and in the face. His shirt is bloodied.* LENA *takes him from* LUCIO. WHORE *enters with a bowl of water and cloth.* LENA *soaks the cloth in water and points at the jar of perfume.* WHORE *fetches it.* LENA *starts to wipe blood from* CARAVAGGIO. WHORE *watches him intently*.)

WHORE: Oh, sweet heart of Jesus! Poor Lello. Do you know something, Lena? He looks a bit like Our Lord. Maybe it's the blood. What happened to you, son? An accident?

LENA: Keep out of this.

WHORE: I was only asking.

LENA: Mind your own business.

WHORE: I'll sit here and say nothing, but I warn you, my stomach turns at the sight of blood. Have you anything I could take to settle it?

(*Silence.*)

May as well be talking to the wall.

(LENA *has removed Caravaggio's shirt.*)

God, you have the stomach of a horse. I couldn't look –

LENA: For Christ's sake, Anna.

WHORE: I know where I'm not wanted.

LENA: You're not wanted.

WHORE: Then just for badness I'll stay.

LENA: Can you raise your head?

(*She examines* CARAVAGGIO's *head for wounds. She fingers his hair. Touching a wound, she makes him cry out.*)

OK, it's not deep. You'll live. I'll clean it.

(*She washes the blood from* CARAVAGGIO's *head. She reaches for the perfume.*)

You'll smell sweet as a baby. (*She applies the perfume.*) It stings.

WHORE: He won't care, because he's a brave boy. Aren't you a brave boy? Aren't you?

CARAVAGGIO: Fuck up.

WHORE: Delightful.

CARAVAGGIO: Get rid of her.

WHORE: Do no such thing, Lena. What harm am I doing? You have some cheek barging into a respectable house and giving two decent women such a shock. I have a good mind –

(CARAVAGGIO *struggles to his feet.*)

Don't threaten me. I'm warning you. I've met your type. A disgrace to their sex. In my day men were men and respected women. Do you hear me, don't come near me.

(CARAVAGGIO *grabs her by the neck.*)

Lena, he's a maniac. He's going to kill me.

(CARAVAGGIO *drags her to the bowl of bloodied water. He pushes her face into it. Releasing her, he holds her head above the bowl and she spews water back into it.* CARAVAGGIO *releases her and staggers to a chair.*)

42

Fuck you, I've had worse done to me, and I'm still not
leaving.

(CARAVAGGIO *laughs*.)

You've made a sudden recovery.

CARAVAGGIO: Speak when you're spoken to.

LENA: What happened?

(*Silence*.)

LUCIO: He –

CARAVAGGIO: Shut it.

LENA: Is anyone dead?

(CARAVAGGIO *nods*.)

Who?

(CARAVAGGIO *shrugs*.)

Who is dead?

CARAVAGGIO: A man.

LUCIO: It was a clean fight. Caravaggio was brilliant. Absolute
fucking magic, honest to Jesus. And the guy who got it had
it coming to him.

LENA: What did he do?

LUCIO: He called us names.

WHORE: What?

LUCIO: He called us girls. He picked the wrong man to insult.
He insulted you too, miss. That really drove your man
there out of his tree.

LENA: How did he insult me?

LUCIO: He called you, well, he said you were . . .

LENA: What? A whore? Lena, the whore? The pride of the
Piazza Navona? Was that it, the insult? Whore?

LUCIO: Yea.

LENA: He was right. And you killed for that?

LUCIO: Tempers were high. They were playing –

LENA: I don't give a damn what –

LUCIO: It wasn't just names. He tried to do us out of some
money for swag we nicked at the Cardinal's house –

LENA: What? What did you take from there?

LUCIO: Toni's gone off with it. He hates violence, so when the
fight got up, he cleared. Better find the bastard or he'll
trade the lot for a bowl of spaghetti.

43

(CARAVAGGIO *laughs*.)

LENA: You fucking idiot. You fucking idiot.

CARAVAGGIO: It was easy.

LENA: It was coming.

LUCIO: He was asking for it.

LENA: Who was he?

CARAVAGGIO: The less you know the better.

LENA: Has he connections?

CARAVAGGIO: I have better ones.

LENA: So, you're safe?

CARAVAGGIO: Not that safe. I'd better leave for a while. I need some money.

LENA: How much do you want?

CARAVAGGIO: Whatever you offer.

LENA: You're in no state to run tonight. Lie low here.

CARAVAGGIO: They'll soon start looking.

LENA: I'll lie.

CARAVAGGIO: Her?

LENA: She's loyal. Him?

CARAVAGGIO: He values his life.

(LENA *moves to exit*.)

Where are you going?

LENA: To inform. All right?

CARAVAGGIO: I need a drink.

LENA: That's what you're getting. (*She exits*.)

WHORE: Lena's a good girl.

(*Silence*.)

You won't hurt her, will you?

(*Silence*.)

I nearly married a man who was killed in a fight. I never recovered. Never.

(*Silence*.)

I was beautiful once. It goes, beauty. The wind takes it. I walked through Rome and I watched the world watching me. They still watch, but I never looked back at them. Beauty.

CARAVAGGIO: The man was beautiful.

WHORE: What man?

44

CARAVAGGIO: The dead man.

WHORE: I never look on the dead.

CARAVAGGIO: Are all dead men beautiful?

WHORE: Stop talking like this.

CARAVAGGIO: I didn't notice how beautiful until I saw his blood. It became him. Flesh and blood. Beautiful.

WHORE: You killed him because he wouldn't have you? You were after him?

CARAVAGGIO: I was following him. Waiting to kill him. All my life. To kill. To die. Maybe he was following me. Finally, we touched.

WHORE: What's a queer doing after Lena?

CARAVAGGIO: What's a hag doing after love?

WHORE: I'm not a hag and I'm not after love.

CARAVAGGIO: I am a queer and I'm not after Lena, but you're after love.

WHORE: What makes you believe that?

CARAVAGGIO: I can see your face. I can tell what has happened to it. You drowned it in wine and you will drown in water. You were never beautiful. You only imagined it. And what you imagine, you believe. But it wasn't there. Beauty. It never was, woman.

WHORE: What would any queer know about women? You hate them all because you weren't born one.

LUCIO: How little you fucking know.

WHORE: I can smell rot off you already.

CARAVAGGIO: The wind didn't take your beauty. It exposed you as ugly. You walked through Rome hoping to be noticed but you were laughed at young and you're laughed at now. You're still looking to be noticed. Well, I have. Do what you have to do with your life. End it. Go to the river. It's where you're wanted, nowhere else.

WHORE: You are death.

CARAVAGGIO: Death, and you are rotten with it.

(LENA *enters*.)

LENA: Do you want a drink?

(WHORE *moves to exit*.)

WHORE: I've had enough.

45

LENA: Where are you going?

WHORE: To rest.

LENA: Say nothing, hear?

WHORE: Who hears a ghost talking in the river? (*She exits.*)

LENA: Anna?

   (*Silence.*)

LUCIO: I better move as well. Pour me none.

LENA: I wasn't going to.

LUCIO: Right, I'll try and find your man, Antonio. If I do, can I
   bring him here for safety?
   (*Silence.*)
   Is that all right?

CARAVAGGIO: Get out.

LUCIO: I'll keep my eyes open, just in case they're already
   searching for you, and report back. All right?
   (*Silence.*)
   All right. See yous. (*He exits.*)

CARAVAGGIO: Drink.

   (LENA *pours wine and hands it to* CARAVAGGIO. *He kisses her
   hand and feels her hair.*)

LENA: It's still wet.

   (CARAVAGGIO *kisses* LENA's *hair. She sits by him, buries her face
   in his shoulder.* CARAVAGGIO *raises his hands to her face, pauses,
   clenches his hands together.* LENA *rises and walks away.*)
   Where will you go?

CARAVAGGIO: Hills, south of Rome. Contacts there from long
   ago. Likely still there. Then Naples. Fucking Naples. They
   eat their young in Naples. (*He howls and laughs.*) Come on,
   Lena. Naples. React. You hate –

LENA: Not in the mood.
   (*Silence.*)
   You'll never come back here?

CARAVAGGIO: No, will you be glad?

LENA: What the fuck does that matter to you, my love?
   (*Silence.*)
   Well?
   (*Silence.* LENA *hands* CARAVAGGIO *some coins.*) Enough?
   (CARAVAGGIO *counts the money.*)

46

CARAVAGGIO: No.

LENA: All that's going.

CARAVAGGIO: No more?

LENA: Not for you. I've got myself to look after.
(*Silence.*)

CARAVAGGIO: I just want –

LENA: What you get. What you deserve.
(*They drink.*)

CARAVAGGIO: My life's gone mad, I've ruined – I've killed – I
paint, I kill.
(*Silence.*)
Lena.
(*Silence.*)
Help me.

LENA: Shut it.

CARAVAGGIO: You can take my belongings.

LENA: Burn them.

CARAVAGGIO: Burn.
(*Silence.*)
Bury.

LENA: The dead.

CARAVAGGIO: Our dead.
(*Silence.* LENA *starts to cradle an imaginary child.*)

LENA: What will we call it?

CARAVAGGIO: Don't call our son it.

LENA: All right.

CARAVAGGIO: No fights about it being a boy?

LENA: If we fight, the noise will waken it.

CARAVAGGIO: Him.

LENA: Let him sleep.

CARAVAGGIO: Who does he look like?

LENA: His father.

CARAVAGGIO: Come on, he's his mother's son.

LENA: No, he's his father's. And he's dead, Lello. The child is
dead.

CARAVAGGIO: No.

LENA: He died. When I wasn't looking he slipped out of me. He
fell.

CARAVAGGIO: It's not your fault.

LENA: I killed him.

CARAVAGGIO: He was born dead.

LENA: Son. My son.

CARAVAGGIO: Lena.

LENA: I wanted him. I wanted a child.

CARAVAGGIO: It's over now.

LENA: Never look at me again. Never touch me.

> (*Silence.*)
>
> I need to walk through the city.

CARAVAGGIO: I'll come with you.

LENA: You'll be caught. We'll be watched. Go to bed.

CARAVAGGIO: With you.

LENA: Fuck off, fuck off, fuck off.

CARAVAGGIO: The child.

LENA: The child is dead. Do you understand? It is dead.

CARAVAGGIO: No. Our son –

LENA: Was never born. You couldn't give me a birth. You only bring death. Isn't that why you had to kill? You want to enter darkness. All you really see is the dark. To give life, you must love the light. You love the dark. Leave me. You're a queer. I love you but you're a queer. See the queer. See his darkness. See yourself. Don't see me. Don't see me any more.

> (*Silence.*)

CARAVAGGIO: I'll leave.

LENA: Stay.

CARAVAGGIO: I'm tired, Lena.

LENA: Stay. Sleep. I want to watch you sleep. The last time. See you dream.

CARAVAGGIO: Can I stay with you?

> (LENA *opens her lap to* CARAVAGGIO. *He lays his head there.*)

LENA: Dream. Dream, son. Dream.

> (*The dream commences.* SISTER, *Caterina Merisi, appears as a ghost.*)
>
> Go to sleep. Dream.

SISTER: Dream, Lello, take me into your dream.

LENA: Sleep, son, your mother is the whore.

48

SISTER: Your mother is yourself.

LENA: Your father is the goat.

SISTER: Your father is calling, Lello.

LENA: The goat and the whore, the dreamgoat and the girl.

SISTER: Who is the girl, did you marry her, Lello?

LENA: It was our wedding, the virgin caught the unicorn.

SISTER: Did you have a child?

LENA: A child conceived to die, and I want to die.

SISTER: Sleep, Lena, leave him. Sleep.
    (LENA *sleeps*.)
    Open your eyes. Brother, do you see me. Lello, my
    brother, look at me.

CARAVAGGIO: Caterina. Sister. Caterina. (CARAVAGGIO *rushes to
    embrace* SISTER.)

SISTER: Keep your distance, Lello.

CARAVAGGIO: Why?

SISTER: Don't kiss my corpse.

CARAVAGGIO: Are we in the grave?

SISTER: No, in a dream.

CARAVAGGIO: Why are you here, sister?

SISTER: I died. Giving birth to my death. The child broke my
    body, Lello. I died cursing my son.

CARAVAGGIO: Gentle sister –

SISTER: Gentle? Ever gentle. Too gentle. So gentle they ripped
    me open to let my husband save his son. Do you remember
    what I was, Lello?

CARAVAGGIO: Silk, you touched like silk, your favourite colour
    was black. If I were rich, I'd buy my sister silk, black silk
    and paint –

SISTER: I wore black. It was my blood. The child poisoned me.
    They cut him out and something spilt over me. I couldn't
    even squeal to stop, but I saw I was covered and it was
    black. It was my blood. I was dying and had I ever done
    any wrong?

CARAVAGGIO: No.

SISTER: Why was I punished? Why did I suffer?
    (*Silence*.)
    I did not die cursing my child. I did not curse his father. I

cursed all children and all fathers and I cursed God for
creating woman.

CARAVAGGIO: For creating man.

SISTER: Show me your hand.

CARAVAGGIO: Why?

SISTER: Show me.

(CARAVAGGIO *gives* SISTER *his hand.*)
Rough hand.

CARAVAGGIO: Never stop working. If I stopped, I'd die.

SISTER: Your hand wants to stop. Your flesh knows what will
kill it. Your work will finish you.

CARAVAGGIO: It's wrong. My flesh is wrong. My body's all
wrong. My mind knows better.

SISTER: What does it know?

CARAVAGGIO: Knows itself. Knows everything. Sees
everything. Lets me paint other flesh. Loves it. Hates my
own. Hates body. Wants body to die.

SISTER: Flesh had a dead son.

CARAVAGGIO: Mind was glad, mind laughed.

SISTER: Mind all right alone.

CARAVAGGIO: Son had flesh like body and body did not laugh at
dead son. Forgive my body.

SISTER: It does what it must.

CARAVAGGIO: Body gets tired.

SISTER: Poor flesh, wants to stop seeing. Wants to sleep.

CARAVAGGIO: And not dream. Not pain. Not all the time.

SISTER: Stop working.

CARAVAGGIO: But mind never stops seeing. I work. I paint. I
paint well. I can prove that. I can call on witnesses to prove
that.

SISTER: Call them.

CARAVAGGIO: Will they hear?

SISTER: They already have.

(CARDINAL *appears, in rags, led by his* SERVANT. CARDINAL
screams.)

SERVANT: Keep your voice down.

(CARDINAL *whimpers.*)
I said enough.

50

CARAVAGGIO: Can he hear us?

SERVANT: He hears nobody but himself.

CARAVAGGIO: Cardinal.

SERVANT: Do you hear the man?

CARAVAGGIO: Eminence.

SERVANT: Answer him.

> (CARAVAGGIO *goes towards* CARDINAL. CARDINAL *screams*.)

CARAVAGGIO: Caravaggio, it's me, Caravaggio. Do you know me?

> (CARDINAL *grunts loudly. The grunts develop into a sound resembling 'bread'*.)

Bread? Do you remember bread? The smell of it? Fresh and brown, like the boys you loved? Do you remember eating? Eating with me? Drinking. Confessing. Do you remember?

SERVANT: Forget it, friend. I've tried often enough to have a sensible conversation with the old bastard. If I have to watch over him much longer, I'll be as cracked as he is. Sometimes he does what you want though. Then he's a good boy, aren't you?

CARDINAL: Good boy. Good boy.

SERVANT: When you're good, you get food, don't you?

CARDINAL: Bread.

SERVANT: You kept me hungry in your palace until you would make up your mind to eat. You fed your whores with good meat. I had the leavings from your table. Look what your whores fed you. You laid them in soft beds. I shivered outside your door, waiting to attend you and your bits of dirty cock. Now you ask me for bread. Here's the bread I have for you.

> (SERVANT *opens his shirt and* CARDINAL *goes to suck his breasts*. SERVANT *hurls him away*.)

CARAVAGGIO: Do you know who you are?

CARDINAL: Good boy, good boy. (CARDINAL *holds out his hand to* CARAVAGGIO.) Good boy, kiss, good boy.

> (CARAVAGGIO *kisses the hand*.)

Holy.

CARAVAGGIO: Who –

CARDINAL: Father.

CARAVAGGIO: Who is holy?

CARDINAL: God. God saw. More than you could see, he saw. Good god. Evil god. God saw good and evil. You saw evil. He saw I hid your evil. God saw me in your evil. And father, holy father, hide me from God. The holy father said, save yourself. Sin no more, sin no more. You, pray for me. Paint no more. Paint no more. Pray.

CARAVAGGIO: Go from me for ever.

CARDINAL: Blessed be the hands that anoint me with iron. Blessed be the tongue that spits curses on my head. Blessed be the feet that walk the way to damnation. Blessed be the eyes that see the same damnation, for they have looked on truth and found it lacking. I have looked on God and found him lacking, Caravaggio. There's nothing there. Nobody there. Not even yourself, great painter. It comes to this. Nothing. No one. Beware the sin of pride, my son. Beware the power of God. But do not believe. Do not believe.

(CARDINAL *and* SERVANT *fade*.)

CARAVAGGIO: Jesus, preserve me. Jesus, protect me. Jesus, preserve me. Protect me.

SISTER: From what?

CARAVAGGIO: A death like that.

SISTER: There are other deaths.

CARAVAGGIO: Whose?

SISTER: Those you'll be remembered by.

CARAVAGGIO: Who?

(LUCIO *appears, clutching a torn blanket to him.*
ANTONIO *appears, his face disfigured.*
WHORE *appears, drenched.*)

WHORE: Caravaggio.

ANTONIO: Caravaggio.

LUCIO: Caravaggio.

ANTONIO: Hear us.

LUCIO: See us.

WHORE: Touch us.

ANTONIO: Paint us, paint us.

WHORE: Tell him.

52

LUCIO: Tell him what he painted, what he touched, he saw, he heard.

WHORE: Do you see me, Caravaggio? You sent me to the river to drown my sorrows. In the river I found a lover who embraced me coldly. I wept for my life and the tears turned me into salt, for I could not dissolve in that water. I did not fight death, I welcomed it, but death did not welcome me. It fought my sinking and I struggled to die, not live. I did not want the life given to me.

ANTONIO: I tried to win you once when I was beautiful. I was afraid to win, afraid someone one night would kill me. He did. He planted something in me that grew. A terrible flower. Sucking the life out of me. A boy with a bowl of fruit. Do you remember? Beautiful boy, his shirt hanging from him, dying fruit in a golden bowl. A boy with a bowl of beautiful fruit. Dying.

CARAVAGGIO: Tell me I did not disease you.

LUCIO: You saw him. You didn't touch him.

CARAVAGGIO: I know your voice.

LUCIO: You knew my face.

CARAVAGGIO: It's different.

LUCIO: It's starved. It died of hunger. I nursed him through the disease. I was known as his bedmate and when he died so did trade. I could turn my hand to nothing else. I starved to death, Caravaggio. My belly killed me. Hungry. I died wasted. Like an old man. Why didn't you save me?

CARAVAGGIO: I couldn't.

LUCIO: You wouldn't.

CARAVAGGIO: Why are you doing this to me? I am innocent of all you throw at me.

WHORE: Drowned.

LUCIO: Starved.

ANTONIO: Diseased.

LUCIO: Your poor, Caravaggio.

ANTONIO: Your models, Caravaggio.

WHORE: Your bread and cheese, Caravaggio.

LUCIO: Your genius.

WHORE: Your reputation.

ANTONIO: Your victims.

WHORE: Better we had never been born.

LUCIO: Better we'd never seen the light of day.

ANTONIO: You put our like in the light.

WHORE: Put us back into darkness.

> (*They fade.*
> SISTER *takes* CARAVAGGIO'*s hands.*
> *Silence.*)

CARAVAGGIO: Let me die, Caterina. Let me die. Show me my death. Let me die.

SISTER: Come home, son. Come home to me.

CARAVAGGIO: Who?

SISTER: I'm here, Lello.

CARAVAGGIO: Mama?

SISTER: Are you hungry, son?

CARAVAGGIO: You died, Mama. I buried you. I put you in the clay. Go from me.

SISTER: My house is empty. Our house. Go and fill it with sons. We need the living in our house.

> (*Silence.*)

Son.

CARAVAGGIO: I filthy your memory with my sin. You know your son. He knows his sin. It is mortal. Go from me.

SISTER: Do you want your father?

CARAVAGGIO: No more.

SISTER: Talk to your father.

CARAVAGGIO: Don't want to see him.

SISTER: Am I a stranger to you?

> (*Silence.*
> SISTER *holds out her arms to* CARAVAGGIO.)

What's wrong, man? Are you too big for petting? I suppose so. I forget easy. I left you early. Why are you crying? Stop. Come to your father.

CARAVAGGIO: No.

SISTER: What brings you home?

CARAVAGGIO: Love. Love you, want to see you. I was too young when you died.

SISTER: But you went on living, and the living mean more than

54

the dead. You belong to them, not to me long buried. Go back. Live.

(*Silence.*)

What I'm saying's the truth, hear me.

(CARAVAGGIO *takes out his knife and points it at* SISTER.)

Too late, son, too late. You may as well put that through your shadow as put it through your father. I'm air now.

CARAVAGGIO: Watch me, father. (CARAVAGGIO *paints the air with his knife.*) This is how I die. How I kill myself. This is how I paint. Living things. In their life I see my death. I can't stop my hand. I can't stop my dying. But I can bring peace to what I'm painting.

SISTER: Then raise your hand in peace. Paint.

(SISTER *takes the knife from* CARAVAGGIO. *He raises his hands. Light rises from his raised hands, drawing* WHORE, ANTONIO *and* LUCIO *from the darkness.* CARAVAGGIO *speaks to the* WHORE.)

CARAVAGGIO: You swallowed a river. They fished you out. You were thrown still drenched into dry clay, wet with sin as we are all wet with sin. Pray for us sinners, now and at the hour of our death. Forgive us sinners, drowned with sorrow for the sins of our flesh, and if I cannot dry your sins, let me dry your flesh.

(*He dries the* WHORE's *hands in his own.*)

Dry.

(*He goes to* ANTONIO.)

A boy remembered his father, holding him. Nobody listened. He banged a gold platter to make the world hear. I heard, I saw, a boy with a bowl of fruit. I fashioned you into a golden bowl and whoever eats from you will be clean for you are without blemish.

(*He wipes the disease away from* ANTONIO's *face.*)

Clean.

(*He goes to* LUCIO.)

I ate from your body. It was good. We laughed that night. You poured wine on me and lapped it. You were a god, a god of wine, and I wanted to drink your divinity, flesh and blood. Grape. God of the grape, great Bacchus, live for ever.

(*He kisses* LUCIO.)

Full. Father, as I speak, I see. As I breathe, I fire. As I love, I roar. I open my mouth. I change colour. Come to me, my animals. Open the cage of silence. Come from the forest of your frame.

(*Light intensifies upon* ANTONIO, WHORE *and* LUCIO.)

WHORE: Who is the bird whose song is golden?

ANTONIO: Lion, roar your lament of love.

LUCIO: Hound, play with the wounded lion.

ANTONIO: Hare, lie with the sleeping hound.

WHORE: Steed, open your trusty mouth.

LUCIO: Dragon, breathe your web of fire.

ANTONIO: Eagle, see with all-seeing eye.

WHORE: Bull, weep for the cows and calves.

LUCIO: Lizard, change colour for ever.

ANTONIO: Unicorn, preserve the species.

CHORUS: Unicorn, protect the species.

(*Music.*

WHORE, LUCIO *and* ANTONIO *move towards* CARAVAGGIO. WHORE *touches* CARAVAGGIO's *hands.* ANTONIO *touches* CARAVAGGIO's *eyes.* LUCIO *kisses* CARAVAGGIO.)

SISTER: Dragon, breathe your web of fire.

Steed, open your trusty mouth.

Lion, roar your lament of love.

Lizard, change colour for ever.

Hare, lie with the sleeping hound.

Eagle, see with all-seeing eye.

Hound, play with the wounded lion.

Bull, weep for the cows and calves.

Who is the bird whose song is golden?

Unicorn, preserve the species.

Unicorn, protect the species.

Unicorn, preserve the species. Unicorn, protect the species.

WHORE: Live.

ANTONIO: Live.

LUCIO: Live.

CARAVAGGIO: Light.

56

(LUCIO, ANTONIO *and* WHORE *fade*.)

Da, I'm scared of the dark. I see things in the night-time. I want a story, I'll go to sleep. I met my sister in a dream. She said she was you and Mama. She told me I was going to die like she died and Mama died and you died. I don't want to die. I want to see you. Tell me a story. Father.

(*Silence*.)

Father.

SISTER: What's wrong with you?

CARAVAGGIO: He left me. You all left me. It's dark. I want a story.

SISTER: There was a boy.

CARAVAGGIO: What happened to him?

SISTER: He was born.

CARAVAGGIO: Where?

SISTER: In the pit of his mother's belly.

CARAVAGGIO: Then what?

SISTER: He fell from it and grew into a man alone, the day his father died.

CARAVAGGIO: Son of his dead father, he ran away to see the world and see himself and paint the two together.

SISTER: If he could paint, he could see and speak for ever without dying.

CARAVAGGIO: He painted darkness as well as light for he came from his father out of his mother's darkness, and he wished to remember, remember what he was.

SISTER: He called what his hands spoke and saw, he called it painting.

CARAVAGGIO: Only in painting can the light darken and the dark lighten.

SISTER: His eyes can't stop seeing nor his hands working; they're workers' hands and in working, in painting they find peace.

CARAVAGGIO: Calm.

SISTER: Peace.

(*Silence*.)

CARAVAGGIO: Shall I die?

SISTER: Not in this dream.

CARAVAGGIO: Then I'll live.

57

SISTER: Live.

CARAVAGGIO: It goes on. I'll live.

(SISTER *fades*.)

Caravaggio.

(*Silence*.)

Michelangelo Merisi da Caravaggio.

(*Silence*.)

Lena.

CARAVAGGIO *lays his head on* LENA's *lap. She wakens. She strokes* CARAVAGGIO's *back, hair and wakens him*.)

LENA: Come on, animal, the beauty sleep's over. Get up, it's nearly daylight.

CARAVAGGIO: What?

LENA: It's daylight almost.

CARAVAGGIO: Right. (CARAVAGGIO *rises*.)

LENA: I've nothing here to eat.

CARAVAGGIO: Want nothing. I'm full.

(*Silence*.)

LENA: Where will you go first?

CARAVAGGIO: South. The hills.

LENA: Then Naples?

CARAVAGGIO: Then Naples.

LENA: Fuck Naples.

CARAVAGGIO: Fuck Naples.

(*They laugh lowly*.)

LENA: A kip.

CARAVAGGIO: The worst.

LENA: Eat their young in Naples.

CARAVAGGIO: They say they're delicious.

LENA: Better get a move on.

CARAVAGGIO: Better.

LENA: They know I know you.

CARAVAGGIO: Not any more.

LENA: Suppose not. Pity.

CARAVAGGIO: Pity.

(*Silence*.)

Right. Go.

(*Silence*.)

LENA: I dreamt I stood in a room, a beautiful room. All bright. Pictures on the walls. All yours. I was in the centre of the room, but I wasn't in the painting. I looked at them and I looked up and I saw you looking down at me. You were happy. It was over. You were at peace. I took my eyes from you and looked around the walls and saw you still in all the pictures. Even if you were gone from me, they were there and you were with them. And I started to laugh because it hit me you were looking at them from above, so you must see them all upside-down, and I knew then somehow we'd won, we turned the world upside-down, the goat and the whore, the queer and his woman.

CARAVAGGIO: Lena.

LENA: Lello.

CARAVAGGIO: Magdalena.

LENA: Caravaggio.

CARAVAGGIO: Last walk in the forest.

LENA: No. Cut down. The forest's gone. No more trees or birds or shapes or colours. The virgin of the forest is a cheap whore and the unicorn's a stupid goat. Jesus Christ, protect the two of them. What are they? Well, this whore's a tired woman and my goat is a broken unicorn.

CARAVAGGIO: I see. That's it?

LENA: You'll live.

CARAVAGGIO: We'll die.

LENA: So we will.

CARAVAGGIO: It won't be together.

LENA: No? Think not? When death comes, no matter where we are, be one alive or not, be one there or not, we will die in each other's arms, and I will shed sore tears to leave you alone. Now fuck off. Run. It's nearly morning. And I know nothing. Nothing. Go. Here. (LENA *gives* CARAVAGGIO *more money*.)

CARAVAGGIO: See you.

LENA: See you.

(CARAVAGGIO *exits*. LENA *clears up the bloodied cloths*. LUCIO's *voice is heard*.)

LUCIO: (*Off*) Missus.

(*Silence*.)
Caravaggio.
(*Silence*.)
Missus.

LENA: What?

LUCIO: Are you there?

LENA: Who are you? What do you want?

LUCIO: It's me, Lucio. I was there earlier. Can I come in?

LENA: Who's with you?

LUCIO: My mate, Antonio. We've got the stuff from the palace. You told me we could bring it here.

LENA: Come in.

LUCIO: Come on.
(LUCIO *and* ANTONIO *enter, dragging a bag of booty*.)
Where is he? Caravaggio?

LENA: Caravaggio? Who's he? Oh yes, the painter. Knew him years ago. Haven't seen him in a long time. No, I can't say I know him now. Wouldn't recognize him even. Do you know him?

LUCIO: Me? No.

LENA: Are you looking for him?

LUCIO: Why should I be looking for him?

LENA: Why should anybody be looking for him?

LUCIO: Oh I see.

LENA: Good. Does he see?

ANTONIO: I don't know what yous two are on about.

LUCIO: It's OK. He's retarded.

ANTONIO: I'm not retarded.

LUCIO: That's a sure sign you are retarded when you say you're not.

ANTONIO: What do you want me to say? I am retarded?

LUCIO: Now you said it. Everybody heard you.

ANTONIO: I'm not fucking retarded.

LENA: Will you two bastards keep your voices down at this hour of the night? And what are you carrying?

ANTONIO: I've been carrying this load on my back ever since the killing –

LUCIO: What killing?

ANTONIO: Your man, the –

LENA: What man?

LUCIO: I know of no man. We haven't seen any killing. Do you remember?

LENA: He remembers, don't you?

ANTONIO: Yes, I remember. Sorry. I'm a bit slow. I need things spelt out –

LUCIO: You see, I told you he was retarded.

(ANTONIO *grabs* LUCIO. *They fight.* LENA *opens the bag of booty. She takes from it a chalice, a gold cross, a silver bowl, and finally a red cloak.*)

ANTONIO: Do you submit?

LUCIO: Never.

ANTONIO: Do you submit?

(LUCIO *screeches.*)

Submit.

LENA: You've done well. Good stuff. Worth a bit.

(*The fight ceases.*)

ANTONIO: How much?

LUCIO: Where will we get the best deal?

LENA: Navona. Let me introduce myself, gentlemen. Lena, a frequenter of the Piazza Navona. I know who to ask. Safely. Come evening. One thing though. This is mine.

(LENA *holds up the red cloak.*)

ANTONIO: How's it yours?

LENA: It belonged to a friend. I'll mind it for him.

ANTONIO: It'll cost you.

(LENA *clips* ANTONIO's *ear.*)

LENA: Will it?

LUCIO: Is that all you want?

LENA: To keep, yes.

LUCIO: Why?

LENA: Memories.

ANTONIO: Who did it belong to?

LUCIO: Your man?

ANTONIO: Where is he anyway?

LENA: Looking down on us, and he sees everything. He sees us now. Yes, he'd like the look of you.

61

ANTONIO: Would he?

LENA: Take your clothes off.

ANTONIO: I beg your pardon.

(LENA *raises the gold cross*.)

LENA: I command you in the name of the Father and of the Son and of the Holy Ghost to get your clothes off.

ANTONIO: But you're a woman.

LENA: I will curse you in the name of Christ if you don't get them off.

(ANTONIO *undresses rapidly*.)

ANTONIO: I've never had it off with a woman.

LENA: God moves in mysterious ways.

ANTONIO: Now what?

(LENA *arranges the red cloak about him, posing his body, placing the cross of John the Baptist by* ANTONIO's *side*.) Weird.

LENA: Weird. (*She admires her composition*.) Yes. Yes. Well, Caravaggio, do you see him? Beautiful, yes? Can you hear me? Can you see us? It goes on and on and thanks be to the sweet crucified Jesus on. See? See. Do you see him, Caravaggio? Do you see? (*She laughs.*
Music.
Light.
The sound of CARAVAGGIO's *laughter. Darkness.*)